Where in the World Is . . . ?

by Mrs. Heitmann's class
with Tony Stead

capstone

A Community

by Danielle and Sara

What is a community?

A community is a place where people play, work, and learn stuff.

My House

by Isabella

Where is my house?

My house is near the grocery store.

Where is my house?

Our School

by Colin and Rebecca

Where is our school?

Our school is in Wilmington near a bakery.

Where is our school?

Our Park

by Molly

Where is our park?

Our park is across the street from the school.

Where is our Park?

The Fire Station

by Asher and Francesca

Where is the fire station?

The fire station is near Bellevue Park.

Where is the Fire Station?

I go up the hill, and then I am there.

This is a fire station.
FIRE STATION 51
51

The Pizza Parlor

by Shannon

Where is the pizza parlor?

The pizza parlor is near the ice-cream store.

Where is the Pizza Parlor?

Where in the world are we?

We are in Wilmington, Delaware.